JUV
FIC

Markham, Marion M.

The Halloween candy
mystery

cop. 1

9.95

DATE			

The Halloween Candy Mystery

The Halloween Candy Mystery

by Marion M. Markham

Illustrated by Emily Arnold McCully

Houghton Mifflin Company   Boston

Printed in the United States of America
P 10 9 8 7 6 5 4 3 2

Library of Congress Cataloging in Publication Data
Markham, Marion M.
The Halloween candy mystery.
Summary: Twins Mickey and Kate use their powers of
deduction and scientific expertise to catch a burglar
on Halloween night.
[1. Mystery and detective stories.   2. Halloween—
Fiction.   3. Twins—Fiction]   I. McCully, Emily Arnold,
ill.   II. Title.
PZ7.M33946Hal   [Fic]   82-6054
ISBN 0-395-32437-8   AACR2

CONTENTS

1

Two Pandas

Mickey's Halloween costume lay on her bed. On her twin sister's bed was another costume. They were both black and white. Well, almost all black and white. Kate's costume had a shiny pink nose. Every Halloween Mickey and Kate had to dress alike. This was Kate's year to pick, and Kate wanted to be a panda.

Mickey wanted to be a detective with a magnifying glass and a curved pipe.

"I know what you're thinking," Kate said.

Mickey said, "I wish Mother would let us be different."

"We *are* different," said Kate.

"But we don't look it."

"Being twins, we get more candy," Kate said. "People think twins are cute. Especially when we dress alike."

Mickey wasn't listening. "If I was Sherlock Holmes, you could be Dr. Watson."

"I don't want to be Dr. Watson. I want to be a panda. You know, they're interesting animals. Not bears at all, but—"

"Or I could be Nero Wolfe and you could be Archie."

Kate said, "Mother's trying to be fair and equal."

"Sometimes being fair is really unfair." Mickey sighed.

"My costume's a little different." Kate held up a small flashlight. "The nose lights up."

"We're both still pandas, though."

"Well, it's too late now." Kate tied a scarf around her hair. She turned the flashlight on and stuck it under the scarf on top of her head. When she put on the costume, the flashlight lit the nose. Kate's eyes looked out from behind the open panda mouth.

The shiny pink nose blinked.

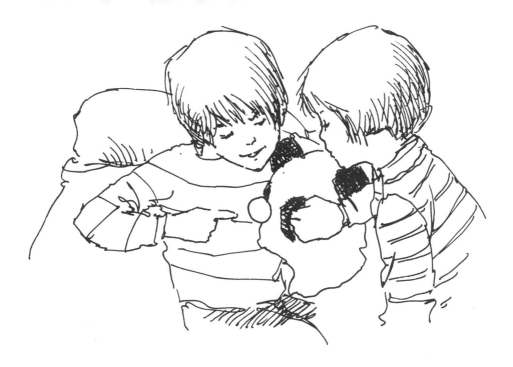

"How'd you make it do that?" Mickey said.

"It's a special bulb." Kate pulled the panda head off. "When the bulb gets hot, a metal strip inside curls and makes the bulb blink off. When the strip cools, the bulb goes on again. It's a scientific fact that electricity makes heat." She switched the blinking flashlight off. "Next year we can be different."

Mickey said, "That's what we thought last year."

"Last year you picked. Policemen. I didn't fuss. Even though the cap was too big and kept falling over my eyes. Now you can be a panda."

Last year, when they had lived on Indian Island, Uncle Corwin had lent them police caps and badges. He was chief of police there. Now they lived in a small apartment, and their panda outfits had come from a big store where all the costumes looked alike.

Kate was ready first. "I'll meet you downstairs, in the front hall," she said.

After Kate left, Mickey looked out the window. Next door was Miss Wink's house. In the back yard was a tool shed and an apple tree. A full moon peeked over the roof, throwing long shadows that made the house look spooky.

A very tall tiger climbed Miss Wink's front steps. His tail twitched as he walked. He made Mickey think of the Pink Panther. Maybe next year she could be Inspector Clouseau. Or Charlie Chan. Or Nancy Drew.

Kate stuck her head in the doorway. She was breathless from running back upstairs. "Slowpoke. All the candy will be gone. A tiger just went to Miss Wink's house."

Mickey said, "I know. I'm just about ready." She picked up her panda head and her orange paper sack that said TRICK-OR-TREAT.

"Where's my trick-or-treat bag?" Kate said.

"Down in the front hall."

"How do you know that?" asked Kate.

"Simple deduction. You've only been two places — the kitchen and the front hall. If you had left it in the kitchen, Mother would have seen it and followed you out."

"You're right. She's always running after us with lunch bags, or mittens, or homework we've forgotten."

"You must have put the bag down on the hall floor. Then, when you saw the tall tiger walk past to Miss Wink's, you hurried back to get me."

Kate thought a moment. "But how did you know I was in the kitchen?"

"We always tell Mother when we go out." Mickey grabbed Kate's arm. "And since you've already told her, we don't need to stop again."

Downstairs, Kate's bag was in the front hall, just as Mickey had said.

2

Fright Night

Outside it was dark. Clouds brushed the face of the moon. Ghosts and witches giggled at the two pandas. Pirates and cowboys stared at Kate's blinking nose.

"Cool," a clown said.

Leaning out of their apartment window, Mother called, "Do you want Jeff to go with you?"

"No," Mickey and Kate said together. Going with a big brother was even worse than wearing the same costumes.

They rang Miss Wink's doorbell.

Ding-dong. The sound echoed inside. But nothing happened.

Mickey rang again.

Ding-dong, repeated the bell.

Miss Wink took a long time to answer. A very long time. "Oh, the Dixon twins," she said.

"How did you know it was us?" Kate's voice was fuzzy. It came from the panda's neck.

"Twin costumes."

Mickey poked Kate. Miss Wink didn't notice. She looked over her shoulder, as if someone was behind her.

"Let's see," she said loudly. "Where did I put the candy?" She opened a drawer. Mickey heard paper crackling. "I know it's here somewhere."

Kate poked Mickey. "How can anyone lose Halloween candy?" she whispered.

"Here we are." Miss Wink dropped a piece into each bag. "How's your Uncle Corwin? I sure would like to see him." She lowered her voice. "Tonight." Her smile was more like a frown.

"Uncle Corwin was just—" Before Kate could finish, Miss Wink closed the door.

"City people are funny," Mickey said. "She knows Uncle Corwin visited us last weekend."

"Forgetful, I guess. She didn't remember where the candy was either," said Kate.

Mickey unwrapped Miss Wink's candy and put it in her mouth. She had to lift the panda head to do it. "Peanut butter taffy."

"Don't talk with your mouth full." Kate unwrapped her piece. It wasn't candy. Inside the orange paper was a ring with a diamond as big as a peanut. It glistened in the moonlight. "Wow," she said.

3

Diamonds and Tigers

Kate stared at the ring in her hand. "Miss Wink made a mistake. She wouldn't give me her ring. Unless the diamond is fake. It could be a Cracker Jack prize."

As Kate talked, Mickey tried to open her mouth. The taffy made her teeth stick together.

"We could test by scratching it on a window. It's a scientific fact that a diamond will cut glass." Kate held the ring up. "It sure looks real. We'd better take it back."

Mickey chewed and swallowed hard. "No. Wait," she said.

"Why? Miss Wink will be worried."

"Don't you think Miss Wink acted sort of strange?" Mickey said.

"Because she couldn't find the candy?"

"And what she said about Uncle Corwin. The way she said 'tonight.'"

Kate nodded. "So?"

"So she was giving us a secret message." Mickey paused. "There's a burglar in her house," she said dramatically.

"How do you know?"

"Simple deduction. Remember how she looked over her shoulder?"

"You read too many detective stories," Kate said.

"Well, she gave you a diamond ring. And Uncle Corwin is a police chief. That sounds like a message to me."

"Why didn't she just tell us?"

Mickey said, "Because he was probably behind her in the hall. And he's still in there!"

Kate thought, then said, "The tiger who was here before. He was awfully tall. Tall enough to be a man."

Mickey said, "If only we could listen at her window. Maybe we could hear something."

"Miss Wink never opens her windows at night."

"I know. She says the night air's bad for her rheumatism."

Kate said, "A very unscientific idea."

"You and your scientific ideas."

"Sometimes they're pretty good. I have an idea of a way we might listen."

"How?" Mickey asked.

"First I have to go home and get something."

"Hurry," Mickey said. "I'll keep watch from the bushes." The bushes were scratchy. But Mickey could see both doors. If the burglar left Miss Wink's house, she'd know.

She hoped Kate would hurry.

"Psst." Kate's hiss surprised Mickey.

"Sssh," Mickey hissed back. "Where are you?"

"Right next to you." Through the darkness, Mickey could barely see her. Kate had switched off the blinking flashlight that lit her nose.

"What do you have?" asked Mickey.

"A drinking glass. If you were a burglar, where would you be?"

"Looking under the mattress," said Mickey. "In stories, older ladies always hide things under the mattress. What does that have to do with a glass?"

"If you put the glass against the bedroom window and your ear against the glass, you may be able to hear something."

The window was over their heads. Kate handed Mickey the glass. Then she gave her a boost up.

Mickey listened. "Hey, it works," she whispered.

Kate asked, "What's happening?"

Mickey put her finger to her mouth as a signal for quiet. After a minute she motioned to be let down.

"Well?" said Kate.

"Someone's there, all right. A man! I think he was asking Miss Wink where she keeps her jewelry."

Kate said, "We'd better get out of here."

"And call the police," Mickey said.

"They might not believe us. It's Halloween."

"You're right. Uncle Corwin says people are always playing silly tricks on Halloween. Go ask Mother to call."

"She might not believe us either."

Mickey said, "Show her the ring. Make a scratch on the mirror to prove it's real."

"Mother wouldn't like that."

"You'll think of something."

"What will you be doing?" Kate's voice sounded worried.

"I'll watch from the bushes."

"Don't do anything crazy."

"I won't. Get going! Before he gets away."

Kate handed her flashlight to Mickey. "Be careful."

Mickey waited. The moon climbed higher, casting deep shadows on the porches. She heard footsteps, and the laughter of boys and girls. Then there was something else. A door opened, pouring light onto the front porch. The tiger came out of Miss Wink's house. As the door slammed, he took off the tiger head.

Mickey turned on the flashlight. The circle of light shone on the man's face. Then the blinking bulb went dark. Before the bulb blinked on again, the burglar was gone.

4

Where's Miss Wink?

Mickey ran to the front of Miss Wink's house. Two policemen, one tall and one fat, drove up in a squad car. Kate, Jeff, and Mother were there too.

"Did you see him?" Mickey asked.

"Who?" said Jeff.

"The burglar. He ran away."

The tall policeman said, "We didn't see anything."

"We were patrolling in the next block when the radio call came in," the fat policeman said. "All we saw were boys and girls in costumes."

"The burglar was dressed like a tiger," said Kate.

"If it really was a burglar," the tall policeman said.

"Ask Miss Wink," Mickey and Kate said together.

They all went to Miss Wink's front door. The fat policeman rang.

Ding-dong, the bell chimed.

No one answered.

The tall policeman said, "Let's go to the back."

Kate, Mickey, Jeff, Mother, and the two policemen went down the front steps. They walked around the house. They climbed the back steps. The tall policeman rang.

Ding, went the back doorbell. Miss Wink still didn't answer.

Mickey turned the doorknob, and the door swung open. On the kitchen floor was a black purse. She bent over to look at it.

The fat policeman said, "Don't touch anything. Fingerprints."

"I know," said Mickey. "No clues here. The purse is empty."

Jeff said, "Where's Miss Wink?"

"Spread out and look for her," the tall policeman said. He went down to the basement. Jeff went to the tool shed. The fat policeman went into the living room. Mother and Mickey went to the bedroom. Kate looked under the dining room table.

Mickey was sure Miss Wink was in the closet. She opened the closet door. There were only dresses, shoes, and hats.

"You're not supposed to touch anything," Mother said.

"How can we find Miss Wink if we don't
open doors?"

"Did someone mention my name?" a muf-
fled voice said. Mickey looked around. An
arm stuck out from under the bed. Then a leg.
In a minute, all of Miss Wink was out.

Mother said, "Miss Wink."

"Call me Amanda."

"Are you all right?" Mickey asked.

"Now I am. When the front bell rang, I thought he'd come back. The tiger, I mean. Then I heard the back doorbell. When the kitchen door opened, I was so frightened! I hid under the bed."

The fat policeman came in. "A sensible thing to do. But why didn't you call us right after the burglar left?"

Miss Wink blushed. She stammered. Finally she said, "I fainted. I know that's silly. No one faints these days. When I was growing up, it was quite proper. I'm afraid I still do it sometimes."

Mother put her arm around Miss Wink. "I'd faint too, Amanda."

"Anyone would," said Mickey.

Kate was behind the fat policeman. She said, "Shock makes the blood leave the brain. It's a scientific fact."

The tall policeman's voice thundered below them. "She's not down here."

"We found her," the fat policeman hollered. He took out a notebook. "Tell us what happened."

"My money is gone. It was in my purse, under the mattress. He wanted my jewelry too, but I tricked him."

Mickey and Kate said, "We know."

"I hope you still have my ring," Miss Wink said.

Kate nodded. "Mickey solved your message about Uncle Corwin."

Mickey said, "Kate thought about listening through a glass."

"I'm confused," Miss Wink said, and she looked it.

"I called the police," Mother said.

Mickey said, "I saw the burglar's face with Kate's flashlight."

"Did you, now?" the fat policeman said.

"Just for a second. Then the bulb blinked."

The tall policeman said, "You'd better come to the station house and look in our mug book." He was in the hall because the small bedroom was too crowded.

From the kitchen, Jeff called, "Miss Wink's not in the tool shed."

As he looked in from the hall, Mickey said, "It took you long enough."

"The door was locked. I tried to jiggle it open."

Miss Wink looked even more confused. "I don't remember locking it. But I haven't used the shed in such a long time!"

"Kate and I are going to the station on police business," Mickey told her brother.

5

Police Business

The station house was very busy.

"Wouldn't Uncle Corwin like to be chief here!" Mickey said.

"I don't know," said Kate. "He wouldn't have time to go fishing, or do so many things with Aunt Mae."

"I guess not. Too many crooks." Mickey was surprised at the number of pictures in the mug book. They all looked alike. Would she know Miss Wink's burglar?

Mickey turned the pages slowly. Everyone watched. And waited.

"Here he is," she shouted. "I'm sure this is the one."

"Kimbo," the tall policeman said.

Kate asked, "What's a kimbo?"

"Not what. *Who*," said the fat policeman.
"We've had trouble with him before."

"Come on, we'll take you home," the tall
policeman said. He held out a bowl of popcorn balls. "Have one."

Kate said, "We're not allowed to eat home-
made treats."

"In case someone's put something funny into it," Mickey said.

The fat policeman said, "My wife made these."

"Oh," the twins said.

"She makes good popcorn balls," the tall policeman said. "It's sandwiches that she puts funny things into."

"Some of us happen to like ham-and-raisin sandwiches," said the fat policeman.

"And peanut butter with raisins, and Swiss cheese with raisins."

"My wife likes raisins."

Kate whispered, "No wonder he's fat. Raisins are full of sugar. It's a scientific fact."

Riding home in the police car, they found that the popcorn balls had raisins too.

6

Kimbo

It was after nine o'clock. Except for the raisin popcorn balls, they'd missed all the treats.

"Can't we please go out again?" Mickey asked, as soon as they had finished telling what happened.

Mother said, "It's too late."

Mickey said, "Even if we take Jeff with us?"

"Well—if Jeff will go." Jeff didn't look as if he wanted to go.

"We'll tell you lots more about the police station," Mickey said.

"And share our candy with you," offered Kate.

"Promise?" Jeff said.

"Whatever we get, you'll get too." Mickey tugged at his sleeve. "Hurry! We don't have much time."

"Time for what?" he asked.

Mickey didn't answer until they were outside. "Time to find the burglar. The police know Kimbo. We know his costume."

Kate sighed. "Too much candy isn't good for us anyway." She didn't sound as if she meant it.

"There's a tiger now," said Jeff.

A yellow and black striped tail disappeared around the corner. They chased it. Jeff was ahead. He had the longest legs.

"Stop," Mickey yelled, as Jeff grabbed for the tiger.

Jeff stopped.

The tiger stopped.

"Miss Wink's tiger was very tall. This one's shorter than Jeff."

The tiger ran away quickly.

"We can't chase every tiger on the street," Jeff said.

"Sherlock Holmes never gives up," said Mickey.

Kate said, "If I had a map, I'd figure how far he could get. I'd draw a circle that far from Miss Wink's house."

"That's dumb," said Jeff. "You don't know whether he walked, took a bus, or drove a car."

"Besides," Mickey said, "we could never cover the whole circle alone."

"What'll we do?" Kate said.

Mickey said, "Let me think."

"She's trying to unlock her mind and find one of her 'simple deductions,'" Kate told Jeff.

"Unlock. That's it," said Mickey.

Kate looked puzzled. "What's it?"

"It *is* a simple deduction, if you just put the clues together."

Jeff said, "You didn't have any clues."

"No, but I think you did. Miss Wink and you."

"Me?" Now *he* looked puzzled.

Mickey asked, "Jeff, what kind of lock was on the shed?"

"I couldn't tell. It was on the inside."

Mickey grinned. "Come on." She ran back to Miss Wink's front sidewalk. "I think Kimbo is here," she said. "At least this is where he was."

"We all know that," Jeff said.

Kate said, "Do you believe a burglar returns to the scene of the crime?"

"I think he never left," Mickey said.

"We searched Miss Wink's house," Kate said. "Where was he?"

"If I'm right, Jeff was warmest."

"The tool shed?" said Kate.

Jeff said, "You told us he ran away."

"He must have cut around the house when the flashlight blinked."

"He wouldn't be here now," said Jeff.

Mickey said, "He might. There was a lot of noise. Police sirens. People shouting. You rattling the door. Maybe he's still afraid to come out."

"Sure," Kate said. "He'd wait until everyone was asleep."

"Science?" Jeff sniffed.

"Psychology."

"Let's investigate," Mickey said. She started

around the side of the house. "I'll pull on the shed door," she whispered. "You two be ready to grab him if he tries to get away."

The moon slid behind a cloud, making the back yard very dark.

Jeff said, "This is dangerous."

"Shhh," Mickey and Kate hissed.

Jeff picked up a fallen tree branch. Kate held her breath. Mickey grabbed the shed door and pulled.

The door wouldn't open.

"I'll get the police," Kate whispered. She

ran to Miss Wink's back door. A few minutes later, Mickey heard a distant siren. The sound came closer. Suddenly the shed door opened. A tall, striped shadow leaped out of the blackness.

Jeff tripped him with the branch. Mickey jumped on him as he fell. She shoved her trick-or-treat sack over his head while Jeff grabbed the tiger's legs. Kimbo struggled free. He ran again, the sack still over his head, and bumped into the fat policeman. Both of them tumbled on the grass.

"Good work," the tall policeman said. He snapped handcuffs onto Kimbo's wrists.

7

Twins Are Different

As Kimbo got up, Miss Wink came out on her back porch. *"Very* good work," she said. "Will you come in for a cup of hot chocolate?"

"I'd love some," Kimbo said.

The fat policeman said, "I'm on a diet."

Kimbo said, "I'm hungry. I've been hiding in that shed for hours."

"We don't have time," the tall policeman said.

The fat policeman leaned over and picked up an embroidered change purse. It had fallen from Kimbo's pocket.

Miss Wink said, "That's mine."

"Evidence. We'll return it later."

Kimbo hung his head as they led him away around the corner of Miss Wink's house.

The twins looked at Jeff. Mother had only let them out because he was with them. Would he make them go home, now that Kimbo had been caught?

"Hot chocolate would be great," he said.

Miss Wink's kitchen was warm and cheerful. The hot chocolate had marshmallows *and* whipped cream on top.

"I don't see how you knew he was still there," Miss Wink said.

Mickey said, "It really was a simple deduction, once you gave me the clue."

"*I* did!" Miss Wink looked pleased.

"You were surprised when Jeff said the shed was locked."

"Well, there was nothing in it to lock up."

Mickey looked at Jeff. "And you didn't see the lock."

"I told you I didn't. It was on the inside."

"A tool shed never has a lock on the inside. Someone on the outside has to be able to unlock it."

Jeff said, "I should have thought of that."

"None of us thought of it at first," said Mickey. She took a big bite of marshmallow.

Miss Wink said, "I've been thinking. I never use that shed. Maybe you twins would like to have it for a clubhouse."

"Super!" said Mickey and Kate.

"It can be a science club," Kate said.

"It can be a detective club," Mickey said.

Miss Wink thought. Then she said, "What about a scientific detective club?"

Kate said, "Maybe Mother will let me have a chemistry set. I can't burn a hole in the cement floor of the shed. If I spill something, I mean."

Mickey remembered that Sherlock Holmes was a scientific detective.

Both girls nodded. A scientific detective club sounded just right.

Maybe Kate would write about their adventures the way Watson wrote about his adventures with Holmes. Mickey hoped she would.

Miss Wink said, "Now I know how to tell the Dixon twins apart. You—" She turned to Kate.

"Kate."

"You, Kate, like science. The one who wants to be a detective is Mickey."

"I like to climb trees, too," Mickey said.

"And I want to be an inventor," Kate said.

Miss Wink said, "Twins just look alike. They're really different."

"We've always known that," Mickey and Kate said together.